Beyond the Cracked Door

E. L. Berkley

ISBN: 978-1-953181-13-8 (Paperback)

Front cover design by Dominique J. Smiley

Printed in the United States of America.

First printing edition 2023.

Published by Happie Face Publishing House, an imprint of Happie Literacy Works, LLC.

contents

DEDICATION

For Julia, Ida, Katherine, Louise, Jean, Ruth, Elora, and Athena.

To my readers: Live a full life so that you may die empty of regret. Unexpressed talent burdens the soul and evaporates the spirit.

Take your swing.

CAN YOU HEAR ME NOW?

J oey kept checking with the hotel's front desk for his mom's arrival. Still no sign of her. The young woman behind the desk gave him a warm smile. Joey barely noticed as his shoulders dropped. He left the desk after thanking the concierge...again. Fighting nerves and disappointment, he headed toward the bathroom. His bladder was full, and his stomach was churning. This was his first year playing varsity basketball, his team was just three games away from the championship title, and his mother was nowhere to be found!

He walked down the long, dismal corridor towards the isolated bathroom. Unlike the lobby, which was currently going through renovations, this part of the hotel clearly hadn't been touched in quite some time. The air was thick and stale. It's as if he could taste the dusty, peeling wallpaper on his tongue. A spider-web thin breeze caressed the back of his neck. He and his bladder jumped simultaneously. A trickle of urine seeped out just as he found the bathroom door. Subtle relief spread through his body as he discovered the bathroom was private.

Cynthia arrived at the hotel in a distracted fluster. She'd been on the phone with her assistant and several agencies for over two hours trying to secure funding for her non-profit. She has had five missed calls from her son in the last hour alone. What doesn't he understand? She told him that she would be there after her meeting. This community center was important. She tried to explain it to him earlier that day. The more she tried to talk to him, the more frustrated she became; it was as if she was speaking to someone with a language barrier.

She checked in, never giving the woman at the counter her full attention. The woman immediately recognized Cynthia. Joey described her perfectly. Not so much her physicality, but her mannerisms. She continued her conference call and gave the clerk her identification. Cynthia only looks up briefly when the woman mentions Joey by name. Obviously, he'd been bugging this woman to death for God knew how long. She made a mental note to apologize for his behavior when she was done with her meeting. *Would a small fruit basket be appropriate? Yes. That would do.* She would have her assistant take care of that detail later. After receiving the room key, she made her way to the ancient elevator. It looked as if it were still being manually operated. She got the feeling a little boy on a tricycle was going to come around the corner screaming, "REDRUM!" at any moment.

Joey headed back to the desk after leaving the old bathroom only partially relieved. The woman offered him a smile with a wink and pointed to the elevator. Joey's eyes shone bright like they did when he was a little boy at Christmas. For a brief moment, he was relaxed, open, and carefree. "Finally, she's here!" He looks at the woman with a smile. He sprinted to the elevator with excitement. "Mom!! You made it." He tried to embrace her.

"I was worried work was -" She stops him with a stiff arm; excitement turns to confusion and then anger. Joey's blood turns to an instant boil. He thinks, *She's still on the fucking phone with her assistant!* He's paralyzed by dejection. Cynthia gave her son a forced smile laced with the undertone of annoyance as the elevator arrived. She pointed for Joey to grab her bags. She continued her conference call, not having realized her son had not moved.

Suddenly, the sound of a heavy, screeching metal door slammed shut somewhere nearby. Joey jumped at the sound and wondered if his mom heard it too. Gravity stretched its tentacles around him as it pushed the air out of the atmosphere. Cynthia whirled around in an unexpected panic. She thought she heard Joey scream followed by a heavy scraping sound. Sweat, the kind only Cannon's theory of "fight or flight" could trigger, started to creep around her entire body like moist, clammy ivy. It rolled across her brow, forging a path down her neck, and infiltrated the valley between her breasts. As the sweat wound like a snake down her back, it began to soak her panties. She gasped for breath. Was the air too thin or too thick? As her mind tried to make sense of what was happening, her eyes locked onto Joey's for what seemed like an eternity. She saw him as if for the first time in ages.

At 14, he's almost 6'3. His once baby face now wrestled with grown man features. The fight was an awkward one. Slightly round cheeks, an impressively defined mustache that met peach fuzz that slowly splattered across a chin more pointed than she remembers. The birdcage of a chest she used to chuckle to herself about now made the ferocious cat on his jersey stand at fierce attention instead of wavering like a kitten on a windy day. Fuller thighs led to chiseled calves. *Where is her little boy?* Her eyes darted back to his. They say the eyes never lie. His big brown almond-shaped eyes betrayed the story his body was telling. Vulnerable, innocent, and scared. *Why scared? What was happening?* Surely, she heard a door slam.

The elevator chime broke the shared trance between the two. Cynthia turned to enter the waiting car as she continued her conference call. Joey was still standing in the empty lobby. He swallowed an angry scream that had been building in his gut. Cynthia snapped her fingers, signaling him to grab her bags. Jaw clenched, he broke out of his stupor, snatched the luggage, and barreled into the elevator. The doors closed with a creaky whine and shudder.

Cynthia continued her conference as she looked for the room key. An old mahogany key chain engraved with the numbers "668" accompanied an even older looking slender iron key. It felt heavier than it should. She turned the key, looking at its intricately carved markings. A distant thought scraped the edges of her mind: why so quiet? For there to be a huge tournament happening, the floor was eerily quiet. However, it felt like someone—or something—was watching, like a cast waiting just off stage from behind an old heavy theater curtain; the kind made of bright red velvet infused with musty dust. The thick air was disturbed by what felt like a subtle breath on her cheek. Cynthia was stunned, which quickly turned to embarrassment. Surely the vent must have kicked it. She scanned the wall to validate her thought, but there were no air ducts or fans to be found. She whirled around, but no one was there except a sullen-looking Joey.

She shook her head several times with a feeble attempt to clear her mind. Four hours of sleep in two days was obviously taking its toll. She also ran out of anxiety medication almost a week ago. She would have her assistant grab her refill when she returned home. Their room was the last door on the left. Old, cracked, and peeling wallpaper dressed the hallway. Several portraits hung on the wall to the left. Velvet curtains and golden braided ropes signified the age of the paintings. The first painting was of a young man in his 20s. His hair was dark, sported a curly mustache, with sharp features and fierce, cold eyes. The portrait was just of the man's face. His stone glare followed her as she passed.

The next portrait was of a beautiful young woman in a stunning red dress. Her thick coarse hair was swooped to the side and cascaded over her tinted shoulder to her waist. Her big brown almond-shaped eyes were friendly, yet drowned in sadness. The lifelike details of the painting bewildered Cynthia. The young woman's cheeks were full and flushed. Her breasts were extremely full. Cynthia then noticed an almost camouflaged bump in the woman's dress, not quite covered by her long tresses. The young woman was pregnant! Cynthia looked back at the woman's eyes. She couldn't help but feel she had seen eyes like this before. Cynthia's mind jolted back to her own son as she passed the third frame, which had a black curtain drawn over it. Joey, with his almond-shaped eyes...

She was still sweating. Her skin was crawling. Was she entering menopause? That would account for the temperature changes and mood swings. Cynthia viciously dismissed the thought. It was Joey and his incessant need for attention while she was trying to work that was the real issue at hand. She walked past room 664. Quiet. No television, no voices...nothing. As she continued, she noticed a slight change in the wall. The pattern was the same, but the colors weren't quite as faded.

Just then, Cynthia felt an acute pain on the back of her heel. She whirled around and screamed, "Watch where the Hell you're going! Damn it!" She immediately regretted the venom she spat at her son. He and her job were the only things in the world she had left. But by the look in Joey's eyes, her job may be the only sure thing. The loud sound of a lock being bolted startled her to the point of jumping. The room key hit the floor with a clatter just out of her reach. She stood frozen, rattled with confusion, and consumed with fear. Cynthia could see Joey read her expression as accusatory. Before she could find her voice, he snatched the key from the floor. She was standing in the same place as he unlocked their room. He flung the door open with such hostility she had never witnessed in him before.

Cynthia was still trying to process what was happening as she headed toward the room. Joey threw their bags in the middle of the floor. He started fidgeting with his basketball, something he only did when he was upset. She noticed a door behind him. The room must have an adjoining suite which would explain the single bed. As she took in her surroundings, she was stunned by the vintage prestige of the room. It had the air of a romantic 19th century fairy-tale castle. However, before she got too enamored with the décor, she needed to talk to her son.

"Joey-" she starts.

"Joseph," he corrected curtly. His eyes were just as dark and cold as his words. Cynthia flinched as though she had been slapped. Truth be told, that's how she felt. The left side of her face was hot and pulsing.

It has been almost 20 years since her first time being hit. Her stomach flip-flopped as she remembered the years of abuse: two miscarriages, loss of intimate friendships, strained relationships with her family. She had even stopped going to church because he didn't like how friendly all the men were; especially that "gold digging pimp" as her ex called her former pastor. It was useless to argue. He even blamed the miscarriages on her working. She quit her job. She had been home a year when she found out she was pregnant with Joey. Something had awakened in her and two things she knew for certain: one, she would never again be a victim of any kind to anyone, and two, he would not kill another baby of hers.

The look in her son's eyes was that of the father he never knew. The knot in Cynthia's gut tightened. She locked eyes with her only child and straightened her back. She spoke with slow precision, "You had better watch your tone, Joseph." She met and raised his challenge.

Joey had never seen this posture in his mother, nor had he ever spoken to her that way. He just wanted her to be present. He didn't want to feel like an afterthought. A voice caught him off guard, like someone had taken over. And "Joseph"? He never used his full name. Some of the guys on the team and his coach had even started calling him Joe. That was cool. It wasn't childish. He dropped his gaze and began to fidget again.

Again, heavy metal dragging against metal could be heard faintly. Joey wondered where the sound was coming from. Maybe it was from the construction crew? Scaffolding? For some reason, it made Joey uneasy. He shook his head quickly to focus himself. He had to tell his mom how he felt, no matter what.

He took a deep breath to muster up his courage, "Mom, we need to talk..."

Before it's too late.

The last four words weren't spoken by him, but he heard them. A chill ran down his spine.

Cynthia was still in defense mode. The last part of his sentence sounded strange. She was convinced that puberty kicked into another gear, hormones be damned. If he thought he was going to make her a victim of teenage disrespect, he was surely about to learn a hard lesson! Cynthia could feel her blood running hot through her veins. She had yet to see a glimpse of his father in his personality. He had never been in a fight. He had never spoken a mean word to anyone. He did well in school and was turning into a stellar athlete. However, she would not ignore in her son what she failed to address with her ex-husband. She'd rather see him—

The sound of ringing interrupted her thoughts. She and Joey looked at each other bewildered. Two phones were ringing—her cell and the hotel phone. Joey stood still while Cynthia pivoted as she tried to locate both phones. To her surprise, she saw a beautiful relic in the far corner of the room on the dressing table. It was pearl white with gold trim that matched the dial and rims of the ear and mouthpiece.

Out of the corner of her eye, she spotted her phone peeking out from underneath the front of the bed. It was probably her assistant. She was instructed not to contact her until Tuesday after the conference call was over unless it was an absolute emergency. Shit! Had something gone wrong with the grant? They were so close. Once the funding was secured, she could take some time off. She was planning to surprise Joey with a two-week road trip down South followed by a two-week cruise to the Caribbean. She needed it...they needed it. But the deal wasn't done yet. She reached down to retrieve her phone. Just as she expected, it was her assistant. The hotel phone was still ringing behind her. She looked up at Joey, who still hadn't moved. It was as if he was frozen. Except his eyes. He was watching her intensely.

Cynthia looked up at her son. "Joey, I need to take this." As she raised the phone to her ear, the hotel phone stopped ringing.

"Hello?" Cynthia answered angrily. Silence.

"HELLO?!" She saw her assistant's name appear on the screen. Just as she was about to speak again, she heard a woman weeping faintly and a man's voice say, "Too late."

Before Cynthia could say anything else, the phone was ripped from her hands. She heard the crash behind her before she was able to process what was happening. It took her about 10 seconds before she found her voice.

"JOSEPH. ROBERT. STEPHENS! HAVE YOU LOST YOUR MIND?!" Cynthia screamed. "What the hell—" Joey didn't wait for the rest.

"You never listen! All you had to do was listen...once!"

He turned around and stalked toward his adjoining room. Cynthia was furious, and for some reason, scared. However, her fury overshadowed her fear.

"Joey! You come back here now!"

Cynthia attempted to cover the distance between them but forgot about the bags in the middle of the floor. As she found herself falling to the ground, she heard the door open to the adjoining room bang open. Cynthia hit the floor with a hard thud.

As she tried to get her foot untangled, she saw Joey's basketball roll across the threshold and disappear. Before she could finish putting the pieces together, the sound of scraping metal pierced her ears. The realization of what just happened hit her like a tsunami.

"JOOOO-EEEEY!"

She finally found her footing and sprinted toward the door where the snap of Fall air punched her in the face.

Inertia almost sent her flying through the door as well. She looked down to see her son about ten feet down holding onto a window ledge. As one crisp white sneaker was kidnapped by gravity, she saw blood pouring from his nose and mouth, but his eyes were clear.

At first, she saw fear. His eyes were screaming. Pleading. Cynthia screamed for help, but her plea was suffocated by the wind. She begged for her son to hang on.

"Joey, baby, don't let go! Mommy's coming!"

In an instant, his eyes go dark and cold.

"Again, you don't listen. Joseph is the name." He released his grasp. Then he was gone. No scream.

Cynthia heard the same metal sounds as earlier. The first sound came when a truck driver below hit the scaffolding as he caught a glimpse of Joey's body falling through the sky. The second sound was the sickening crunch his body made as it hit the empty industrial sized metal dumpster below.

· · · ● · ● · · · ·

"So, can you explain how Ms. Stephens and her son gained access to this part of the hotel?" asks Detective Martin.

"Detective, I just don't understand. The original part of the hotel has been closed since 1985. This is the first day of renovations. I think it should have been torn down, but the Historical Society got involved," the manager rambled.

"Sir, I don't need a history lesson. I need to know how this boy and his mother were able to check into a closed hotel.

"We had signs posted everywhere. I guess with the wind being so high, some were ripped down, but there's still one on the door. My staff and I have been swamped with the basketball tournament and several conferences.

Cynthia overhears the manager.

"*YOUR* STAFF GAVE US THE KEY!" Cynthia's voice is hoarse and frantic. Her eyes are wild and blood shot red.

"*YOU* GAVE US THE FUCKING KEY!"

Her "well put together" boss persona completely dissipated as she lunged at the manager. Several officers had to restrain her as she fell into an out-of-breath heap on the floor.

"Ma'am, I know this is an overwhelming tragedy, but please calmly try to tell us what happened. Start with describing the woman behind the counter."

"I -well...I was on a conference call for work," she stammered.

"Well, that explains why she didn't see the sign," the manager said smugly to one of the officers standing nearby.

Detective Martin shot both the manager and officer a stern look. The officer walked the manager further down the hall and Detective Martin encouraged Cynthia to continue.

"Everything happened so fast. The young lady was very pleasant. She had nice eyes and thick, coarse hair. She may have been mixed. I don't know. Creole?"

After completing her statement, Detective Martin had Cynthia escorted to the morgue.

"Martin, are you ok?" asked an officer.

He stared at the portrait of the small family. The man and the woman seem to be opposites. His eyes were stone cold, while her eyes were soft and kind. However, the boy, maybe three years old, captured his attention. He has an uneasiness in his gut that he couldn't identify. The boy's eyes looked familiar. Brown, almond-shaped eyes that look like they've seen more than his toddler frame...

"Martin? Are we clear?"

A shiver ran through Detective Martin's body, and he began to sweat. An officer placed his hand on his shoulder.

"Martin, are you okay?" He shook his head.

"Yeah, I'm okay. I think I'm finally coming down with the flu. The wife and kids just got over it. I guess it's my turn. Let's get out of here. We're clear."

MASQUERADE

P aulette lit her last lavender scented candle before she lowered herself into the jacuzzi. She created a mental shopping list as the hot water excited the silky liquid she poured earlier into the bubbles: lavender candles, lavender bubble bath, mango butter...

The sting of the hot water interrupted her thoughts. Pain and pleasure started to confuse her. Her sensitive skin demanded the balance of cold water. However, that request was shallow as the skin itself. Her nipples slowly tightened as the temperature of the water increased. Paulette slid down and opened her legs to welcome the rising water. Her iPod changed to "The Secret Garden." A smile slowly spread across her face as she licked her full lips. The light from the candles slowly danced with the beat of the song. Meanwhile, the rhythm of her heartbeat and clitoris were throbbing in sync.

Shit! No more batteries. She added that to her mental shopping list.

"I wonder if I can add a man to this list too," Paulette questioned out loud.

On cue, the hot water thrashed over her pulsing flesh. A teasing shudder ran through her entire body. The water finally rose above the jets. She turned the knob on the tub. Hot water hit her body from every angle. Paulette moved closer to the jet directly in front of her.

Marvin Gaye was also in need of healing as moans of pleasure turned into violent watery thrashes. She let out a pleasurable moaning scream laced with pain as Jodeci pleaded to talk. Paulette sank into the bubbles as the pulsing subsided... for now.

Early the next morning, she went to the grocery store. Her favorite candles? Check. Double *and* triple "A" batteries? Check and check. Scanning through her physical list, she realized she forgot toothpaste.

"Damn it," she said under her breath.

The health and beauty aid section was on the other side of the members-only club. As Paulette made a sharp turn, she nearly ran down a woman she didn't know was there.

"Oh my God! Miss, I'm so sorry. Are you ok?"

"Yeah, I think you just nipped my shoe..." The woman trailed off. "Paulette? Paulette Morris!"

Recognition swept over the pair as they started to laugh.

"Jocelyn Peters. I'm having the strangest feeling of déjà vu." The women giggled.

"Yeah, so is my Achilles heel! It's been almost 19 years since you ran me over in the bookstore on campus and yet it feels like...*today*!" They broke into a laughing fit again and embraced one another.

"Girl, I'm so sorry. Just trying to get everything on my list and out before this place gets crazy."

"True!" they said in unison, breaking out into hysterics again.

Suddenly, Jocelyn stopped short. Her entire demeanor changed, and she took a step back. The animated woman from 10 seconds ago completely disappeared.

"Jo-Pete?" Paulette started toward her old friend when a curt voice from behind her cut in.

"Jocelyn." Spoken with correction and... was that a hint of warning? Paulette whirled around to see another familiar face.

"Manny? Manny Robinson. Wow, what a surprise..." Paulette is interrupted.

"It's Emmanuel. No longer Manny. Just like this is Jocelyn. *Not* Jo-Pete. We're also known as 'The Robinsons.'"

Paulette stood still until a slow realization hit. "Oh? OH!" She looked quickly back and forth. "Oh my God! Congratulations!" The feeling in her gut betrayed her words. She reached out to embrace Jocelyn. However, Manny had already closed the distance and drew her in a protective stance.

"My wife and I have come a long way together. Jesus Christ is now Lord, Savior, and Ruler of our lives."

As Manny slipped into a rant like testimony, Paulette studied the woman that used to be her closest friend. In college, Jocelyn looked like she was always ready for an interview or photo shoot. Girls in the "in" crowd could not stand her. Jo-Pete was beautiful without trying. She wore little to no make-up, had flawless smooth skin, big beautiful bright eyes, and was curvy in all the right places. She also held academic *and* sports scholarships. In addition to having the number one record in her track and field events, she also made a name for herself playing intramural softball. However, it was her personality that truly made her fabulous. Even though her resume was off the charts, there wasn't a conceited or haughty bone in her body. She was humble, graceful, and a little naïve. The latter was well hidden unless you really got to know her.

The woman standing before Paulette looked like a poor knock off of her former bestie. Her skin had lost its natural sheen. Her once thick, long, healthy hair was now damaged and thinning. All sense of style was also gone. Jocelyn looked bland: no traces of color or jewelry–just black, shapeless clothing. Her eyes delivered the biggest shock of them all. The big doe-like, almond brown, star bright eyes were now dark and dismal. Paulette's stomach turned. There seemed to be a memory that was just out of her grasp...

"Paulette?" Manny's voice snapped her train of thought. "Have you accepted Jesus Christ as your Lord and Savior?"

She stood stunned in the aisle. Other members were starting to stare at them. Paulette felt flushed and overwhelmed on the inside but remained cool on the outside.

"Yes. I have. However, I haven't had a church home in years."

"That's unfortunate." He reached into his wallet and handed her a card that said "Deacon Emmanuel Robinson" with his phone number and e-mail.

"Contact me when you're ready to come back into the fold." His expression was smug, and his tone dripped with judgment.

Paulette felt a flash of anger. *Who the fuck did Manny think he was?!* She felt as though her blood was literally going to come to a boil and run out of her ears! She forced herself to calm down. Something was wrong here...seriously wrong.

"Jo-uh...Jocelyn. Call me when you get time. I could use some woman-to-woman fellowship." Paulette dug out her own card and attempted to hand it to her friend, but Manny took it.

"Honey, I forgot the maple syrup. Please get it." His words sounded endearing, but they were encased in ice. Jocelyn's head snapped up abruptly, and her eyes darted back and forth briefly. "It's in the back of the store."

She moved so quickly Paulette didn't have a chance to say anything else.

The warehouse was now in full swing, and the aisle was crowded.

"Manny, it was great seeing you again. I've got to go before I'm late for my appointment." Paulette made a quick turn and was gone before he could respond. She dashed up the main aisle and found a lane that was just opening. She already had the cart set up for the cashier. The young woman rang up her items quickly. Paulette thanked her and darted to the exit. She wanted to hurry to the car so she could watch "The Robinsons." She felt fiery butterflies in the pit of her stomach.

Twenty minutes had passed. Paulette was going through her memory banks when the realization struck.

"Shit!"

Just then, she saw Jocelyn and Manny walking across the parking lot. Once they reached the black Mercedes, he went straight to the driver's side and slammed the door. Paulette was hoping that Jocelyn would still skip the cart shelters like she used to. She watched her friend put all the groceries in the trunk. Paulette gripped the steering wheel, seething with anger.

"That bastard! He really didn't help her," she yelled at the windshield.

Jocelyn walked the cart to the cart shelter. For a split second, she slowed down, but quickly changed her mind. She was headed back toward the building. Paulette jolted with excitement and hit her head on the visor. She flipped the visor closed, hopped out the car, and ran into the opposite door of where Jocelyn was headed.

She arrived about two seconds before Joc. An elderly woman was in the process of wrestling with a line of carts when Jocelyn offered hers.

"Joss!" Startled, she jumped almost a foot. Paulette knew she had very little time. "What the fuck was that all about?!"

Jocelyn looked stunned.

"Never mind. I know you've got to go, but please call me. We've got to talk. I hope you're still good at remembering numbers on the fly. My number is still the same one from college. I live 15 minutes from here in Red Creek Village, Unit 2."

She hugged her quickly. Jocelyn gripped her back and ran out the door.

She had barely buckled her seat belt when she felt a surge run through her body.

"What took you so long?!" Manny had the stun gun aimed at her leg, poised for another hit. This was his favorite torture tactic. Fortunately, her body had adjusted to the voltage so all she had to do was swallow twice before answering.

"I took the cart back like I always do. It was crowded and an elderly woman was having a hard time with a cart, so I gave her mine. Then, I helped her get her walker in."

Emmanuel studied her face for five seconds. He then gave her a kiss on the forehead. "Satan's been very busy today. We must make sure he does not get a foothold lest we perish."

• • • • • • • • • •

18 Years Earlier

Paulette and Keith had been friends since day one of college. She quickly picked up the ambiguity of "they" and "their" whenever the subject of dating came up. So much for her small crush. Friend zone it was. Keith was brilliant, compassionate, cute, and closeted! He was careful, but she knew. However, she cherished their friendship so deeply she wouldn't dare bring it up. It would be during the homecoming of their sophomore year that Keith would come out. He didn't just quietly come out–he *danced* out during the Lip Sync Battle. It was epic. The joy and relief in that dance was pure, albeit short-lived.

Paulette and Jo-Pete were in the Student Union with the outgoing SGA president, Iyan Patrick, discussing logistics for the upcoming fashion show. Keith ran for vice president and won by a landslide. Paulette spotted him in the SGA office looking seriously stressed. She turned to Jo and Iyan.

"Hey guys, I'll catch you later. Joss, fill Iyan in on what you can. I'll see you back in the apartment."

Paulette walked over to the SGA suite to check on her friend. She announced herself with soft concern.

"Knock knock."

"Oh my God, Lettie. I tried calling your apartment ten times. I left four messages. Why can't we be rich and have cell phones?!" Hysteria was building as Keith paced back and forth with nervous energy. Paulette cut in and stopped him mid pace.

"Breathe. Now I know this is serious because one, you *know* I hate being called 'Lettie', and you're the only one that can get away with that shit and two, you *hate* leaving voicemails. What's wrong?"

Keith broke out into gut wrenching sobs. Paulette quickly shut the door and locked it behind her. With her heart pounding, she gripped Keith into a hug.

"Keith, baby, what is going on?" His body shook uncontrollably. "Breathe with me, OK? In... hold. One, two, three...out. Again..."

Keith was still crying but calmed down after a few minutes of this exercise.

"He tried to rape me."

Paulette froze in shock. All the moisture evaporated from her mouth in a matter of seconds. She managed to force out a low rasp.

"What? Who?"

Her mind was jumbled with confusion. The floodgates of her saliva broke open and caught in her throat. She rushed to the water cooler as she felt strangled from the inside. She gulped down two cups before she poured one for Keith. They sat in silence while he sipped slowly on his water. After a few minutes, Paulette found her regular voice.

"What happened? Who...?" She locked eyes with her close friend.

An overwhelming sense of dread was piling up, and it felt like a ton of cement in her stomach. Tears streamed down her face. She recognized the vulnerability and genuine fear in Keith's eyes. Not only did his fear stem from the actual event but also from worrying if he'd be believed. Paulette gripped Keith into another hug. They both sobbed with mutual understanding. Another ten minutes went by before either of them gained composure.

"So, how do you want to handle this? File a report with Public Safety and the Dean's office?"

Keith looked totally defeated as he spoke. "Oh Lettie. I can't do that."

"If they don't believe you because you're gay-"

He quickly cut her off. "No. It's not that simple. Heaven knows I wish it were that simple." Paulette sat in genuine confusion. "Honey, I stirred up quite the hornet's nest when I came out. I knew I'd encounter some closet cases, but I didn't know it would be like *this*!"

Paulette felt an uneasiness in her gut. "Like what? I don't get it. You're acting like you stumbled onto a cult or something."

Keith sat stone faced and replied, "That would be far easier to deal with, Paulette. I'd actually prefer if they were religious zealots like the dude in Waco, or followers of a murderous sociopath. The Closet Society has the ability to be *all* of that...and more."

"The *WHAT* society? You- does that mean what I think it means?"

Keith nodded. "Mostly Black and Latino men. There are a few white boys, but they're carefully chosen."

For the next two hours, Keith told Paulette everything he knew and experienced. The President of the college, the head of security, several local police officers, professors, admissions counselors, and at least 30 current students were all a part of TCS.

"I rejected them. They didn't want me to come out. Manny was supposed to be my 'closet buddy.' Not in a sexual way, but we were supposed to take on certain projects together. It's all about building a power base. Mentoring is the public objective. However, scouting for new members is always the ultimate goal."

· · · · ● · ● · · ·

Jocelyn sat with her hands folded on her lap and eyes down as he liked. She was very careful in her countenance not to reveal her thoughts. Seeing Paulette awakened something inside of her. This was not the life she deserved. It was time to stop being scared and ashamed.

Red Creek Village... Red Creek Village... she replayed over in her mind. She almost forgot to keep her stoic look when she thought of Paulette's phone number. The number spelled out "Hot Sexy One." It was an inside joke of theirs that never got old. She had to fake a coughing fit to hide her giggle. Manny didn't seem to notice. He had that faraway look which meant he was probably thinking of someone else. She knew. She had always known...

· · · · ● · ● · · ·

Paulette raced back home. She knew the phone call she had to make. This was going to get messy, at least for Manny. If the cards were played right, no one–including

Manny—would know the sources of the bombshell about to drop.

Keith had disappeared from social media, and for good reason. He was now the Dean of Students at NYU and taught Psych 101 on Wednesday nights. She knew it was a risk, but to her surprise, he picked up on the first ring. It was as if he had been awaiting her call.

"Keith Garnet. How may I help you?"

"Dean Garnet."

"Lettie?!" They both erupted into laughter.

"Keith, why are you in your office on a Saturday?"

"I wondered the same thing. Now, I know why. I'm waiting for my new phone to arrive in the mail. Did you try my cell first?"

"No. Something just told me to call your office first. Hopefully, this is a good sign. I need your help."

"Hmmm…I'm intrigued. What's the mission?" This used to be their favorite line in college when there was the slightest hint of a challenge in the air.

"It's Manny."

There was such a long pause Paulette thought the call had dropped.

"Hello? Keith?"

His mouth went bone dry. The lightness and melodic rhythm in his voice disappeared when he was able to find his voice,

"Who has he hurt?"

Paulette replayed the bizarre encounter.

"Those bastards! They did it! They really fucking did it!" Keith exclaimed with a strange mixture of disbelief and knowing.

"Did what?! Who?" The fiery butterflies were back once again.

"The Society. I never thought they would really go that far. Oh my God...Jocelyn. Had I known..." Keith broke down crying. "Lettie, I just wanted to be free and live my life. Had I known they would target Joss, I *never* would have left."

Paulette felt hazy on the other end of the phone. She staggered toward the couch where she landed just about the same time that she lost her ability to support her body weight.

"Manny was trying to convince the Dean of Keys to let him test a psych theory..." Keith was cut off by Paulette as the world came back into focus.

"Ok. Hold up. What's the Dean of Keys?"

There was a twinge of paranoia when Keith spoke again, "He has tremendous influence. His job is to know *every-thing* about each one of us. I mean *e-ver-ything*. I wouldn't be surprised if he knew when my father had his first wet dream."

If not for the seriousness of Keith's voice, Paulette may have laughed. However, she knew this was not a joke.

"So, tell me more about this theory," Paulette pressed.

Keith took several deep breaths before he spoke. Seemingly trying to calm himself and gather courage all at once. "It's basically a twisted version of what generally happens to people after a traumatic incident; withdrawn, mistrust, shame...you name it. The trauma is the wild card though. Manny felt if the right person were chosen then the response would be guaranteed."

"But you can't control trauma. Right?" Keith's silence made Paulette grip the phone until it felt like it became one with her hand. She started to feel clammy all over as she lost her ability to speak.

"Lettie, do you know what happened to Jocelyn after graduation?"

"We lost contact for a while. I was going to grad school, and I don't know...life happened. I got a few calls from her, but I was so stressed that first year."

"She was gang raped," Keith blurted out as tears streamed down his face. "I heard about it after it happened, but I didn't connect the dots to who did it until you called."

Keith broke into uncontrollable sobs. Paulette sat stoically on the other end of the phone. All kinds of feelings and emotions bombarded her psyche.

She stuttered, "H-h-he wouldn't..."

With solemn surety, he proclaimed, "He did! I *know* he's behind this!! I just have to prove it!"

"Keith, this is dangerous, and I don't just mean Manny himself. He's a powerful person in the Christian community. If this isn't done right, our lives will be ruined."

"I understand, but I know his weaknesses. Are you up for a house guest? I think it's time to take a short leave of absence for a family emergency..." Keith sounded determined and focused.

"Sure. When?"

"I'll be there tonight."

"Ok, I'll be here. Red Creek Village, Unit 2."

"Got it."

The phone fell out of Paulette's hand as she slid from the couch to the floor overcome with emotion.

• • • • • • • • • •

Manny pulled up to a lush property sprawling with acreage. The house was in stark contrast to the scenery surrounding it. A quaint cape cod was situated out of view from the road. A volunteer from the church helped maintain the bountiful landscape by appointment only. He didn't allow anyone to come to his home without his permission or presence. Packages were delivered to the post office box along with the mail. He and he alone checked the mail and paid the bills. The house, car, bank accounts, and all utilities were solely in his name. After all, the Bible does say the man is the head of the household.

"Put the groceries away and come to the bedroom immediately!"

"Yes, Emmanuel. Right away."

She kept her voice soft and her eyes down. Jocelyn had not seen her husband this agitated in a very long time. This was going to hurt more than usual...

Manny's trance was only broken by the powerful surge of climax and rage. Jocelyn cried silent tears of pain while in the familiar humiliating position.

"Go clean yourself!" He spit the words at his wife as if she were the cause of the excrement and blood. "I expect my lunch when you're done. You have five minutes and not a second more." He was irritated and unsatisfied and decided to cut her usual time in half.

Jocelyn quietly got up and went into the En-suite bathroom. It didn't matter that he gave her five minutes instead of ten. She had learned to do her clean up routine in half the time a long while ago. She would have normally spent that extra time looking at herself in the mirror trying to recognize who stared back at her. But not today. Seeing Paulette had really made him angry.She opened the bathroom door exactly at the five-minute mark. To her surprise, he was still in bed...watching the door. The look on his face was intense with a hint of uncertainty. He tried to mask the latter.

"Is there anything I can do for you before I start your lunch?" She asked with her head slightly bowed and eyes cast downward; trying desperately to sound normal. Silence. However, she dared not move. She knew he was studying her. After what seemed like an eternity, he said,

"Praise the name of the Lord! Satan has not gotten into our home. You've remained steadfast in your obedience. No, I do not require anything. You may proceed."

Jocelyn cleaned up when he was finished with his lunch. Manny went into his office as he normally would spend 3-4 hours preparing for Sunday's service. She was in the laundry room ironing his underwear when Manny appeared in the doorway. Despite being startled, she didn't let it show, but the shock caused her to roll the iron over the back of her hand. Although she felt the searing pain, she never flinched or missed a beat.

"Was your lunch not fulfilling?"

For a brief second, he was the one that looked startled. "No." He straightened his back and said, "No. I've been called for an emergency intercession."

"Oh goodness! I'll get my bible and oil right away," Jocelyn replied as she started to unplug the iron.

"That won't be necessary. Due to the nature of the situation, the brother has requested all men to intercede."

His words didn't totally ring true. She continued ironing, hoping that he wouldn't be able to tell she knew something was off.

"Continue your usual routine. I won't be here to eat dinner. However, I expect you to still prepare the usual. You're also to have yourself ready for service in the morning."

Jocelyn's heart skipped a beat. *Morning? He never left her alone overnight. He barely left her alone at all. Why now?* As if on cue he provided an answer.

"This is going to require serious spiritual warfare. This demon will not go quickly or quietly. Again, I expect you to continue with your routine, especially prayer. Nothing changes. Understood?"

"Yes, Emmanuel."

They both stood still for what seemed forever. He walked over to where she stood. She turned toward him with her head still bowed. He leaned down to kiss the top of her head.

"Good girl." Manny reached down and picked up her burned hand. "Pray," he commanded softly. She did so immediately. She was deep in fervent prayer when everything went white.

As the room started to come back into focus, she realized her perspective had changed. There was also a strange smell lingering in the air. Manny stood over her, gripping the taser. As the fog cleared, the immense pain in her made itself known.

"Amen." He declared as if he couldn't smell her burning flesh or the urine and bowel that permeated the air.

Without helping her up, he repeated, "Amen..."

"Amen," she replied weakly.

He turned and started walking away. "Make sure there are two coats of polish on my shoes. I want you in your navy pinstripe suit tomorrow." He began to whistle.

"Yes, Emmanuel."

He never looked back. She didn't move until the whistling faded.

· · • • · • • · ·

He arrived at the hotel just as the sun dipped beneath the horizon. He pulled up to the valet in front of the hotel and grabbed his bag out of the trunk. A member of the hotel staff approached him to take his luggage. Manny threw a glare that stopped the bellhop in his tracks, and the man turned on his heels and scurried back into the hotel lobby.

He started to walk away from the hotel once his taillights disappeared into the depths of the garage. The massive buildings blocked the leftover heat from the setting sun, making it feel unseasonably cold. An icy shiver slivered down Manny's spine. He saw construction barriers and caution tape as he neared the closed part of the hotel. Years ago, this was the only part that existed. Over time, the hotel expanded, and the original part was used less and less. However, it had been closed for renovations for a long time. The head of License and Inspections was a part of TCS as was the President of the Historical society. They made sure this part of the hotel stayed closed to the public. He barely noticed mixed in with the caution tape was also police tape. He vaguely remembered hearing there had been some type of accident where a kid died recently.

He slowed down and looked around as he approached the entrance. There were no signs of hustle and bustle over here. Still, he felt like someone was watching him. He grabbed the handle with such force that he barely missed hitting himself in the face. The old door let out what sounded like a sigh as it opened. As Manny entered the lobby, he heard a hissing sound behind him. This made him jump and break out into a mild sweat.

"It's just the door, Emmanuel." The voice was both cool and amusing.

"Oh! I mean. Of course." He tried to regain his composure.

"The meeting is downstairs, Manny."

He felt his anger rise and was about to make his correction when he locked eyes with the man behind the desk. The man's eyes were fierce, dark, and cold. What the man lacked in height was definitely accounted for in his eyes. Manny's throat locked up with dryness. *Who was this guy?* He must be a part of TCS otherwise he wouldn't be here. He must also rank pretty high too for him to have called him "Manny."

"I'm afraid you have me at a disadvantage. You know my name, but I haven't received yours," Manny said, trying to match the man's tone.

Clearly, the man found this amusing and laughed. He laughed for what seemed like five minutes. Manny struggled to keep his glare going. Just when he felt it was about to slip, the man stopped laughing.

"Joseph."

"Well, that's better."

Before Manny could say anything, Joseph repeated, "The meeting is downstairs." He gestured toward the old elevator.

He did not like the feeling of being dismissed. He started walking to the elevator. After a short while, the car arrived.

He stepped in and as the door closed, he said, "Thanks...Joe."

As soon as the door slammed shut, the car plummeted downward. He swore he heard Joseph laughing as he tried to fight through the piercing fear that was stabbing him. Just when he thought the elevator was going to slam to the ground, it came to an abrupt halt. Sweat dripped from Manny's forehead as he struggled to regain his breath. He stared at the door. Nothing. He anxiously moved the old school lever back and forth. Nothing. Just as panic was about to set in, the bells chimed, and the door slowly opened.

Manny didn't move. He was utterly paralyzed with fear but was unsure of why he was so scared. He hadn't felt this way since he was a kid. A shiver ran through him as he imagined old skeletons trying to escape their stuffy catacombs.

The door gave a squeal as it began to close on him. Manny quickly snapped out of his paralysis and ran out into the dim hallway.

. . . ● . ● . . .

Jocelyn let the hot water run over her as she watched the shower clock. One minute left. At the five-minute mark, she reached up to turn off the shower. She hesitated. She was alone. When was the last time she had a long, hot shower?

She inhaled deeply and turned the water on full blast. She grabbed the shampoo and started to wash her hair. The pain in her hand seemed to subside as she massaged her scalp. Slowly, her head awakened to the attention. Jocelyn felt as though she were shedding an unwanted exoskeleton. The water ran over her face and into her mouth. She was surprised at the saltiness it held. It was then that she realized she had been crying. That realization broke the levee to the dam of tears that had been building for years.

Jocelyn cried uncontrollably as she slid down the wall of the shower. She cried tears of pain. She cried tears of sorrow. She cried tears of pity and self-loathing. As the water ran cold, she cried tears of anger. She reached up to turn off the water. The tears were gone by the time she reached the mirror. She looked at her reflection. For the first time in years, she saw glimpses of familiarity.

She tore through the house like a tornado, but with the precision of a surgeon. She gathered all her important documentation. To her relief, it was where she remembered it to be. Jocelyn paused when she came across her marriage license. She had always believed in the sanctity of marriage. She had even remained a virgin until...

Jocelyn forced back that thought that threatened to paralyze her as it had done for years. She wiped the tears that she reluctantly shed and folded her marriage license into her Bible. Jocelyn packed a small bag of clothing and some toiletries. She got to the front door and took one last look around. To the naked eye, everything looked in place. Perfect.

· · · · ● · ● ● · · ·

Keith and Paulette must have cried for an hour after he arrived. To aid in regaining their composure, she put on a pot of coffee. Keith brainstormed how to take Manny down. The problem was staying off TCS' radar. Getting on their bad side could get messy. He wasn't worried about himself, but Lettie and Jo-Pete didn't deserve their wrath. God knew Jo-Pete had been through enough. Just as he began fighting back tears, Paulette's phone rang.

She was looking at the phone with that skeptical look you give when you don't know who's on the other end. Then recognition slowly crept across her face. Her alma mater was calling. Probably the annual giving campaign. She sighed. *I guess she could give $100 or so,* she thought. Paulette cleared her throat, "Hello, this Paulette." To her surprise, there was a lot of background noise. She couldn't make out who was on the other end of the line. Then she heard someone crying.

"Paulette?! Paulette, please come get me!" Jocelyn sobbed.

"Oh my God! Joss, where are you?" She placed the phone on speaker so that Keith could hear in case she missed something.

"I-I'm in the student center," she sobbed tears of anxiety and relief.

"*Our* student center?!" Keith asked, astonished.

"Yeah...I'm at the information desk. Please hurry," she pleaded.

Keith was already opening the front door.

"Joss, we're coming right now," Paulette said as she held back tears.

• • • • ● • ● • • •

Manny took a few moments to catch his breath. The excitement of his pending meeting overrode the warning feeling in his stomach. It had been a long time since he met with the guys this way. John, Tim, Paul, Jesse, Jose, and Scott. All of them had been friends since his college days. Most of them were a few years older than he was and had graduated at the end of his freshman year...except John. They sat next to each other at Freshman Orientation.

However, TCS had a way of bringing like-minded people together. One event, in particular, sealed their bond forever. Through their cooperation, Manny was able to test and prove his theory. In turn, he helped establish them as upstanding members in the community. They were the first members of his church. As the church grew, they all became part of the leadership team. There was no part of the church that didn't begin or end with one of the seven.

However, appearances were very important to growing a church. Scott and Jose were still able to pull off the bachelor phase. The rest of them had already gotten married with Tim, Paul, and Jesse having children. He shuddered with repulsion. He couldn't discern what was worse, children or the act of having them. Fortunately, he only had to have conventional sex for the first year he was married to Jocelyn. Honestly, she was easy to discipline. The trauma from the rape already made her reluctant, so she wasn't ready for two months. He only had to play loving, supportive, romantic husband for five months until he knew he had her mind, body, soul, and spirit. He gradually introduced what he really wanted. Once she gave in to that, the rest was a breeze.

It had been so much easier in college to not be seen with a steady girlfriend. He flirted and danced at parties, went on a few dates here and there. He knew once TCS assigned Christian religion as his sector of work, then he would have to take a wife. Fortunately for him, Jocelyn had been the right target to prove his theory and create the proper public appearance. He smirked as his lower member responded in kind.

He found the meeting room at the end of the hall. There was no noise. *Good.* The room was supposed to be sound-proof. The Elders of TCS ordered them to always change the locations of their meetings to which the Keeper of Keys would make sure they had access. He looked around for the object they always used to hide a key in. He spotted a box tucked behind the old hot water heater. Under a pile of dirty rags was an old cigar box with a key inside. The key was old and heavy. He wondered just how old it was. He shrugged, took a deep breath, and opened the door.

A tantalizing red glow was cast throughout the room. The smell of cigarette smoke, cologne, and fervent sweat immediately stirred his loins. Clearly, the meeting was already in full swing. He was pleasantly surprised to see a hot tub in the corner. This had been his long-standing request. It had been agreed upon that every one of them could bring two of their favorite kinks, and all would engage. They had everything from suspension contraptions to latex and bondage. The hot tub was the second part of his fetish; the first was tucked away in his pocket.

Except for the standard sounds that usually accompanied their meeting, there was no talking. The only talking that was permitted was if specific orders needed to be given. Manny silently undressed. He took out the small stun gun and placed it on top of his bag in the corner opposite the hot tub. Since everyone was already engaged in their own activities, he relaxed in the inviting water.

He was thinking of all the ways to use his stun gun when the lights flickered. A flash of annoyance rose in him just as the flickering stopped. Just as he began to relax again, he felt an aggravated thump followed by an aching throb.

"Arg!" Manny growled.

The lights flickered again, and he swore he heard the door open. It sounded heavy, almost vault like. He got out of the hot tub and grabbed the stun gun.

"Punish them. Punish them all," a voice told him. The voice was cold.

Manny stopped short and slipped. No one seemed to have noticed. He got up angry and throbbing more than ever. His eyes were fixated on the door in which he entered. He walked over and tested the handle. Still locked. He looked around the room once more.

"Yes. Punish them." The voice was more urgent this time.

He looked at the group. Only Scott and Jose looked like they were finishing up, so he grabbed two blind folds and barked, "You two! Hot tub."

The men obeyed and got into the hot water. Manny walked over and blindfolded them. He then placed a gag ball in one of their mouths.

"Be creative," he said to the pair with evil flirtation.

"What are you waiting for? DO IT! Punish them!" The lights flickered. *"Maybe I was wrong about you, Manny."*

He felt a surge of rage. The light near the hot tub went out.

"My name is *Emmanuel*!"

He stalked over to the bondage station. Manny raised the stun gun and zapped Jose in the neck which dropped him to his knees with only a small grunt. No one seemed to notice. He zapped him in the neck again, which left him sprawled out on the floor like a starfish. Manny knelt down as his penis throbbed like never before and zapped him in between the legs. It was at this point, Jose lost consciousness.

Manny then grabbed the jar of liquid latex and some rope. He briefly stroked the erection of unsuspecting Tim that was also blindfolded and tied to the chair.

"Almost my turn," Manny whispered.

He flipped over Jose's limp body on the floor and put him in a hogtie. He then placed a bondage mask on him. Finally, he poured the liquid latex over the entire mask, sealing it.

He walked back over to Tim, who was still blindfolded and tied to the chair. Manny snapped his neck with ease.

He heard laughter in the distance but was too excited to focus on it.

Manny eyed the suspension station. Its design required two people that completely trusted one another. Using a basic weight pulley system, each man would use his weight to lift the other.

Manny smiled broadly.

He walked over and tasered Jesse in the neck several times. He dropped so fast, Manny narrowly missed jumping out of the way. The rest went smooth as silk. The rope went taut, and at lightning speed, snapped Paul off his feet. He was just high enough to where his big toe barely brushed the floor. He writhed in brief surprise, then agony, then silence.

Four down...two to go. Manny made his way over to the hot tub. The light fixture just to his left flickered again. The air in the room seemed to get thinner as he closed in on his last two targets.

"That's right. Finish it!" the voice encouraged maniacally.

John let out an overwhelming cry of ecstasy just as Manny climbed the first step. A giant wave of water washed over the steps as he was caught off guard and lost his balance. He cried out and tried to throw the taser, but it suddenly felt as though someone else's hand clamped down over his. Manny panicked as he fell headfirst into the hot water.

Hearing Manny cry out startled John, and he fell backwards out of the hot tub. He ripped the blindfold off his face as he scrambled to his feet. Standing 6'6", he slammed his head into the low hanging light, and crashed backwards onto the floor unconscious.

"HA-HA-HAAAAAAAAA!!"

Back in the hot tub, Manny and Scott were stunned as they groaned in pain. Manny had caught Scott right in the balls when he fell in. The 30K volts from the taser was just enough to daze the wet pair. Manny tried to clear his blurred vision, but all he could make out was a fuzzy red light.

"Well, it looks like you're not exactly who I thought you were, Manny." Joseph's voice seemed to be everywhere in the room.

"I guess your training wasn't thorough enough. You're still just a scared little boy. Oh well, I can still get something from this."

With that, the chain that held the red light snapped and fell into the tub.

. . . .

Jocelyn, Paulette, and Keith had been up all night. They talked, cried, and prayed. Keith told Joss everything he knew and what he had pieced together. They all decided it was best not to "out" the entire TCS. That would prove difficult and dangerous. However, Jocelyn had a plan.

The three friends pulled onto the sprawling grounds of the megachurch. The parking lot crew had already gone inside. Jocelyn instructed Keith to pull right up in front of the door. She had not bothered to shower or change. No more hiding.

"Just stand in the back," Jocelyn instructed.

Paulette and Keith looked at each other with uncertainty but nodded.

Jocelyn bowed her head in a brief silent prayer, took a deep breath, and hopped out of the car. She headed through the main lobby that led to a smaller area outside of the main sanctuary. Her stride was determined and resolute.

"We thank you for your patience. It seems that the leadership breakfast before service ran over. Please continue to engage in private worship," Jocelyn heard someone say and immediately stopped short. Keith and Paulette nearly tripped over her.

"He's not here. Neither are the other leaders."

"Who are the others, Joss?" asked Keith.

She ran down the names. When she mentioned John, Keith snapped at attention.

"What's his last name?"

"Pierceson. Why?"

Before Keith could explain, Jocelyn had already made the connection. She turned on her heels and stalked toward the pulpit. She almost made it to the steps when the head usher tried to stop her. The woman did not recognize her.

BEYOND THE CRACKED DOOR

"Good morning, Margie."

Margie Pierceson looked confused at first, then stunned. She stuttered, "G-g-good morning, First Lady. I-I'm sorry I didn't—" John's wife floundered.

Jocelyn interrupted, "It's fine. I just need to make an announcement."

"Of course," said Margie, still stunned and confused.

Keith and Paulette stood by the door in the back looking apprehensive.

The sanctuary was quiet as a graveyard. The former warehouse had been transitioned into a sprawling space, complete with a second-story balcony. There was no sign of its former function. It truly looked like an old school church with dark wood arches, organ pipes that ran up the wall behind the pulpit, and two areas for the mass choir and music ministry. The church seated a total of 1,500 people in the main sanctuary with another 1,000-person occupancy between the Teen Sanctuary and Children's Church. They also ran two full Sunday services and were considering adding a third.

Jocelyn scanned the congregation. She saw everything from big southern style hats and skirt suits to sneakers and jeans. However, they shared the same look of puzzling shock.

"Good morning. I just overheard that Pastor and the leadership team are running late. That's actually perfect, and it makes what I have to say easier." She took a deep breath and told her story. She ended with the events of the previous day.

"I know some of you don't believe a word I said. I understand. I didn't believe I was actually living it."

Suddenly, there was a wave of murmuring. Jocelyn noticed people were turning around. Her eyes immediately locked onto Keith as she saw him moving closer to the figure staggering into the sanctuary. Paulette grabbed him by the arm.

Jocelyn saw her whisper something in Keith's ear. He stopped advancing, but still looked furious. A few of the men from the parking lot crew approached the man. However, they backed off shortly after. The figure continued to approach the pulpit.

"John!" Margie gasped as she approached the staggering man. "What happened? What is going on?!"

He whispered in her ear, led her to her seat, and kissed her forehead.

Jocelyn looked at Keith and Lettie who still stood at the back. Paulette began moving forward, but Jocelyn shook her head. Paulette paused, but with obvious concern. She watched as John limped up the steps. His shoulders drooped and his head bowed more and more as he got closer to Jocelyn. He stopped about three feet from her. John raised his head slightly, eyes averted, and mumbled something. Jocelyn looked over the congregation and then handed the microphone to the battered man in front of her.

John began in a slow, rambling fashion at first. It seemed he was mostly speaking to himself. He suddenly turned to Jocelyn.

"I'm sorry for what we did to you."

At that moment, Margie jumped up and ran out of the sanctuary sobbing. She nearly knocked over a uniformed officer that had just entered in the back.

"It looks like my time is short. Let me finish this." He sighed loudly. "They're all dead. Manny killed them."

He then dropped the microphone and collapsed on the stage.

· · · · ● · ● · · ·

The entire congregation was in an uproar as more officers began to fill the sanctuary along with emergency medical staff. The latter approached Jocelyn. She allowed them to look her over. The police had taped off the lower Sanctuary and set up a perimeter to stop members of the church from approaching. She noticed John handcuffed to a gurney being escorted by two police officers. Other officers worked to clear the rest of the building. As the medical staff wrapped up, a tired-looking man walked up.

"Mrs. Robinson? I'm Detective Martin…"

THE GIFT

E leanor was stone faced as she and her sister Ruthie stood on the auction block. The bidding was about to begin. Girls their ages would have normally been sold long ago. Eleanor had just turned thirteen. Ruthie was eleven. Both were results of the routine rape of their mother, Cora, by the plantation master. Beau David Lee was infatuated with young Cora from the time his unit invaded the Native's territory. He had instructed his men to kill all male heirs- even children. All women and resources would be sold or traded accordingly. Anything not deemed useful was burned.

But Cora...Cora was not up for debate. Only after baring his first child less than a year later would he learn that she was just barely thirteen. She was tall and curvy. Her skin was that of a biscuit fresh from the oven—lightly golden and glistening like butter. Cora's high cheek bones popped with rosy prominence as her jet-black hair tumbled in waves behind her. Her eyes were fiercely resolute and dark like pure onyx. Her eyes and body almost seemed in opposition to one another. The body seemed young, but the eyes... There was something about her eyes that said differently.

As the auction began, Cora looked out of Master Lee's bedroom window. She locked eyes with her eldest daughter. She gave Eleanor a slow nod. In response, Eleanor squared her shoulders, straightened her back, and gripped her sister's hand tighter. A single tear rolled down Cora's face. However, the fact the girls were kept together as per the master's orders was a sign of how he felt about Cora. It would also probably be one of his last instructions.

Mr. Lee laid on his deathbed. The retired military lieutenant turned real estate mogul had been struck with fever and a severe cough for almost a year. Years earlier, he decided to renovate his mansion into a hotel for soldiers. Three weeks after the project was completed, he fell ill. There was nothing more the doctor could do. The fact he lasted this long was curious to everyone... except Cora and Eleanor.

Unbeknownst to him, Mr. Lee had also assisted in prolonging his life and Cora's. His seed did more than just make children. However, the choice had been made. If Cora wanted her daughter to have a better life, then she had to remove the protection that had been afforded her by her bloodline. It was time for the gift to be fully passed on. No two women could fully take advantage of the gift at the same time. The decision was easy, albeit painful.

Eleanor was strong, stronger than Cora even. The gift was drawn to and exuded a certain kind of strength. As she watched her daughter lock eyes with a slave master, she flashed back to the day she was born. It was the dead of winter at the height of a major storm when her grandmother and mother brought Eleanor into the world.

All had gone quiet. So quiet that Cora thought something was wrong. The baby was not crying. Panic set in until she saw her grandmother's face. As a female elder of their tribe, she delivered all the children. She smiled as she passed the infant to Cora. She received her cautiously, slowly drawing her to her chest. She was startled at what she saw. Eleanor's almond-shaped eyes were locked on her. "Quiet Hawk." Her grandmother kept the tribe tradition by naming all female heirs.

· · · · ● · ● · · · ·

"SOLD!" The word snapped Cora out of her memory. The transaction was complete and now Cora's descent started. Eleanor looked back up at the window one last time. She was met with the same look. She knew...they both knew.

"Until later, my Quiet Hawk." With that, Eleanor and Ruthie were hauled away.

ACKNOWLEDGEMENTS

Anthony: What are the chances of us having this cosmically orchestrated connection? Yup...100% because we're *living* it! I thank you for your friendship, partnership, and leadership. The type of love you have for me is trans-dimensional. It has allowed me to see myself as the version God originally created, instead of the one the world tried to destroy. 143WAO

Ashley: Thank you for allowing me intimate access to your life and holding me accountable! You are perseverance personified–"Straight like that!"

Kera: I would have to dedicate an entire book just to begin to express the impact our sisterhood has had on my life. Your light has gotten me through some extremely dark places. You covered me in prayer when my faith was running on fumes. May every good seed you've ever planted come and overtake you with generational harvests!

La Kesha Joy: Thank you for showing me, in real time, what it looks like to walk in faith! You have had the same love for me since we were kids. Your smile and spirit rival the sun! Thank you for loving the raw me and reminding me who I am.

Shawna: How do I encapsulate our relationship with mere words? I can't. The type of sisterhood we have is anchored in deep water. Being an intercessor is certainly a heavy gift. You wield it well with style and grace! Thank you for covering me. Remember what I said though...

Ebony: *Who knew?!* (Inside Joke) Yet, here we are. Thanks for your support and patience over the past 20 years.

Kris B.: Here's to respecting differences, encouraging shenanigans, and going down rabbit holes since 1997!

D. Odell Benson: You helped to reignite my passion for writing! Thanks for being so selfless (and funny) even in the midst of your own storms.

Dearricka: Just when I thought my sister circle was complete...here you come with the slow stroll! I'm SO honored to have you in my life. Every woman needs a ride or die cheerleader like you in their corner. I pray I am that for you also. WE. WIN!

V&S Lanes: Thanks for being family! The space you have created has allowed me to decompress, grow, and gain clarity when life's fog hits.

Wayne: You literally saved my life. You were the first man to speak of my value, and not try to destroy it. Thanks for "adopting" me!

Tanya: THE RAM IN THE BUSH! God dropped the mic when He connected us! This project would have withered away without you. Your spirit allows women like me to be their authentic selves, no matter how rough and raw. Thank you for accepting me, encouraging me, praying for me, and being the big sister I needed.

Happie Literacy Works: You know how to bring correction without destroying one's spirit. Thank you for making my dream come to fruition!

ABOUT THE AUTHOR

E.L. Berkley was born in Philadelphia, Pennsylvania, the only child of Elihue and Elora. Tragically orphaned by the age of 5, she was then reared and educated in Clayton, New Jersey by her maternal grandmother, Jean. Unbeknownst to the small child, she would be the last chance for redemption for her grandmother who had suffered her own string of tragedies, including the loss of 2 children. The loss of her parents triggered a succession of traumas in her young life. At just six years old, her toy box was thrown away by her overbearing grandmother. Literature and music became the catalyst for her escape route from a harsh reality. This is where she fell in love with writing horror, fantasy, romance, sci-fi, and psychological thrillers. Some of her favorite authors growing up included V.C.

Andrews, Stephen King, Maya Angelou, Anne Rice, and Edgar Allan Poe, to name a few.

At age seven, E.L. would fall victim to sexual abuse, which she would endure for four years. This abuse led to her early teen years being very dark. Rage brewed and churned throughout her whole being. She did not like being a victim and decided that she would never be again. Many missteps ensued. The mentality was right, but the execution was wrong. Her grandmother, though strict, never gave up hope and continued to drill the importance of education, good character, and perseverance through life's challenges.

In addition to her grandmother, there were several teachers and mentors that lit her path as she made her way out of the darkness. She attended the Pre-College Institute at Rowan University in the summer of 1999. The motto for her class was: *From Normal to Extraordinary: Excellence without Excuse!* This program provided not only educational, but emotional and social support needed to build on the foundation her grandmother laid. She received her Bachelor of Arts and Master of Arts degrees at Rowan University in Glassboro, New Jersey.

Made in the USA
Columbia, SC
10 September 2023

22706348R00048